SNOW BEAST COMES TO PLAY

What?!?

PHIL GOSIER

Roaring Brook Press
New York

For Mom

Published by Roaring Brook Press
Roaring Brook Press is a division of Holtzbrinck Publishing Holdings Limited Partnership
175 Fifth Avenue, New York, New York 10010
mackids.com

Library of Congress Control Number: 2016058268

ISBN 978-1-62672-519-5

Our books may be purchased in bulk for promotional, educational, or business use. Please contact your local
bookseller or the Macmillan Corporate and Premium Sales Department at (800) 221-7945 ext. 5442 or by
e-mail at MacmillanSpecialMarkets@macmillan.com.

First edition, 2017
Book design by Andrew Arnold
Printed in China by RR Donnelley Asia Printing Solutions Ltd.,
Dongguan City, Guangdong Province

1 3 5 7 9 10 8 6 4 2

Have **YOU** ever met a snow beast?

Snow beasts only come out in the snow. They have enormous heads, gigantic bellies, and great big feet.

Some like to nap.
SNOOORE!

Some complain it's cold!
BRRR-R-R!

And some wonder why they have bigger feet than everyone else.

HMM.

But this snow beast was different.

This snow beast didn't want to nap.

He wasn't cold.

And he didn't want to compare feet.

This beast wanted to **PLAY**!

So he decided to do something
snow beasts almost never do.

He decided to make a friend.

Snow Beast never had a friend before. But he knew friendships should always start with "Hello."

He knew that for sure.

Unfortunately, snow beasts
can be very LOUD.

He saw a man moving snow . . .

Snow Beast knew
friends should always
help one another.

SNOW BEAST

WANT TO HELP!

WAAAUUGH!

Unfortunately, snow beasts are shockingly large.

He knew it was important
to try to join in!

Uh-oh.

SNOW BEAST SORRY!!

MOMMY! MOMMY!

Unfortunately, snow beasts are a little clumsy.

Snow Beast had tried his
best . . . but nothing worked.

Snow beasts are **LOUD**.
And **LARGE**.
And more than a little **CLUMSY**.

But when they're sad, they're just like you and me.

They cry.

SNOW BEAST WANT PLAY!

ALL FRIENDS RUN AWAY!

He only wants to play!

I still think we should RUN!

Penny imagined how she would feel
if no one wanted to play with her.

So she decided to do something
nobody else had done.

She made friends.